T0147059

My Journey with
GOD
in Spite of the Devil

Memoirs

CLARICE BURTHEY CRUDUP

MY JOURNEY WITH GOD IN SPITE OF THE DEVIL MEMOIRS

iUniverse books may be ordered through booksellers or by contacting:

iUniverse
1663 Liberty Drive
Bloomington, IN 47403
www.iuniverse.com
1-800-Authors (1-800-288-4677)

Because of the dynamic nature of the internet, any web addresses or links contained in this book may have changed since publication and may no longer be valid. The views expressed in this work are solely those of the author and do not necessarily reflect the views of the publisher, and the publisher hereby disclaims any responsibility for them.

Any people depicted in stock imagery provided by Getty Images are models, and such images are being used for illustrative purposes only. Certain stock imagery © Getty Images.

ISBN: 978-1-5320-7240-6 (sc)
ISBN: 978-1-5320-7239-0 (e)

Library of Congress Control Number: 2019903714

Print information available on the last page.

iUniverse rev. date: 06/17/2019

Acknowledgments

First, and always first, I give thanks to my Heavenly Father for giving me the courage and determination to complete this book. Special thanks is given to Sylvia Dianne Beverly, Joyce Williams-Graves, Frances Young, and Willette Warner for encouraging me to write this book and put my story out to readers. These special ladies showed so much support that they motivated me to complete this book. They said they knew my writing this book was within my qualifications.

Thanks also to Pastor Anton T. Wesley, who used his free time—which I know he has very little of—to write words of inspiration to be included. His words inspired me and I know will inspire other readers. His inspiration gave me so much courage as I worked on this special project.

The individuals who took the time to support me with their comments and photographs are greatly appreciated. These added quality to the presentation of my first book, with my life stories that God wanted me to tell.

Finally, I must acknowledge the sincere assistance and help of the IUniverse publishing Company and the devout professionalism shown by their many employees. To my patient family, this would not have been possible without your understanding and encouragement. I thank you. Of course, I give all the glory for my accomplishment to God endowing me with His merciful and miraculous grace. Amen!

Introduction

I was born in 1941 in Durham, North Carolina, to my parents, Rember Odell Burthey Sr. and Ruth Mae Hodges. I had two siblings, Rember Odell Burthey Jr. (the oldest child) and Grover Cleveland Burthey (the youngest). I was the middle child. I came from a broken home. My father and mother were divorced, and we children lived in Durham with my father and my uncles and their wives in a funeral home.

My father was in school to become a minister, and at night he would come home to us children, usually with ice cream or some change as a treat for us. He'd wake us up and give it to us.

Chapter *1*

One day Dad came home with his new wife, Mildred, from Burlington, North Carolina. Dad had completed his schooling, and he was a Methodist minister now for the Colored Methodist Episcopal (CME) Church, which today is called Christian Methodist Episcopal Church. His ministry was governed by a bishop, and the rule was that he had to move every four years to a different church location. After leaving Durham, our first location was Raleigh, North Carolina. Four years later, we moved to Spartanburg, South Carolina. We kids were always the new kids on the block and in school. My first realization that someone could be jealous of me happened when a girl in my class who sat behind me cut off one of my two long plaits. I was about seven years old. I hit her and got in trouble with the teacher, who sent me to the office and called my dad. At the time, the teacher had not seen the girl cut my hair. My dad was called, and he reported the girl's act to her father, who supposedly disciplined his daughter for her act.

Chapter 2

My dad was very resourceful as a minister, and he didn't mind stepping outside his routine. He started a nursery school at our church. Most of the children who enrolled were the children of church members. The nursery school received certain foods, including cheese, powdered milk, eggs, and peanut butter, and the costs were subsidized by the state, so this was mostly what Dad's children ate. This saved our dad money.

He also started an adult typing class in our church. When I was young, Dad allowed me to take typewriting in that class. Little did I know that I would one day become a typing teacher as my first career; however, when I did pursue that career, my dad was deceased. I often wished that he had known how my taking that typing class had developed my interest in typing and thus helped me start my career. He would have been proud to know this.

Four years later, we moved to Montgomery, Alabama, where my father was pastor of another church. I remember clearly that he used to talk about his friendship with certain civil rights activists and other well-known pastors in Montgomery.

Chapter 3

E verything was going fine until one day a group of people stopped by the house for a conference with Dad and talked to my father at length about church and Christian matters.

The conference lasted about two or three hours before ending. About a day or so later, my dad started yelling, "Confusion! Confusion! Confusion!" My siblings and I were so frightened and embarrassed because we thought some of the people in the neighborhood could hear him.

My brothers and I were at a loss about what had upset him so. In addition to the conference, Dad wasn't living up to the standards of a minister when it came to drinking. From time to time, he would have one of us kids go to the store and tell the cashier that we were there to pick up the meat for Reverend Burthey. One day my brother Grover dropped the meat package, and instead of meat, a bottle of liquor broke. He had to tell Dad what had happened, and we were never sent to the store for his meat again. Then a few times when we kids were in bed, he and Mildred would go into the kitchen. After a while, we could hear her saying, "All right, Reverend, get up, and let's go to the bedroom." We could hear him stumbling and knocking against tables and chairs because he was drunk. I would get very scared that he was going to fall and hurt himself or her. That's why today I avoid anyone drinking in excess. I feel that drinking in moderation is all right, but I don't like to be around anyone who might lose control of themselves. So between the drinking and the conference, he had become mentally ill, and we had to pack up and travel back to Durham. But this time our paternal grandmother, Mama Susie, told Dad that we could live with her. I was so nervous and upset when it became obvious that my dad was losing his mind. He had always been my hero. He was so brilliant, and he was a talented singer. He always showed intense love for his three children, although he firmly believed that if you spared the rod, you'd spoil the child. If we did something wrong like lying or being disobedient, he beat us with his belt until we turned black and blue. The worst beatings to us were when he made us take off all our clothes and get in the bathtub. Then if you moved around, you would hurt certain parts of your body. If he had beat us like that in this day and age, he would certainly be locked up if one of us called the police. Knowing this, I do believe either one of my brothers or I would have reported him to the authorities. I still felt that he loved me best since I was his only daughter. In addition, I was the only girl in his two brothers' families. Each of his two brothers had only one son and no daughters.

Chapter *4*

Dad was a thirty-third-degree mason. He took lessons and became a pilot, and he had flown me to Durham and back from Alabama. He was also exceptional and innovative as a Methodist pastor. I remember he used to always begin his sermons by singing a heartfelt song that really kept the congregation alert, interested, and motivated to wait for what was coming. I didn't know then what was going to happen to him or to our family. When my father became progressively mentally ill, he was admitted to a mental hospital. Dad's wife, Mildred, returned to Burlington, North Carolina to live with her mother. My father was stable enough while out of the hospital on a pass, and he made arrangements for us children to live with our birth mother, Ruth Hodges, who was now Ruth H. Sessoms, as she had married Mr. Samuel L. Sessoms of Portsmouth, Virginia.

Our paternal grandmother, Mama Susie, loved my oldest brother, Rember Jr., so much that she didn't want him sent to our birth mother in Portsmouth. Instead she wanted him to live with her. So he remained with her in Durham, and my younger brother, Grover, and I were sent to live with my mother in Portsmouth. My father, who was out on a pass from the hospital, told Mom that he would put us on a bus to Portsmouth, and he relayed the day and time she should meet us. I knew my dad was sick when he got in bed with me one night at the funeral home and reached over in the dark and said, "Come on, Mil." I jumped out of the bed and ran into my brothers' room and got into bed with them. I told them what had happened, and they were understanding. A day or so later, Dad returned to the hospital, never to be released again. He was only thirty-one years old, and he was diagnosed with a serious case of schizophrenia.

My mother met us at the bus terminal, and we went to live with her and "Mr. Samuel," as we called him.

Mr. Samuel and my mother seemed to have an average relationship. But with my room next to theirs, I heard them arguing from time to time. He treated Grover and me just fine, though, and he didn't seem to hold it against us that he had to share his home with us. He worked at the navy yard in Portsmouth, and just like clockwork, he was up at about four o'clock every morning, getting ready to go to work. He was home around four o'clock every evening.

It seemed that all he expected of her was to have his dinner ready every evening and always have his specialty served with the meal—two or three pieces of fried corn bread. Later I would help prepare that corn bread as I helped prepare his meals. Once, my maternal grandmother, Mama Minnie, moved in with us, and she would prepare his meals when my mom had to work late. She taught me how to set the table with a fork on the left of our plates and a knife and spoon on the right. She was a Church of God member and one of the kindest women I'd ever met in my life. She prayed for us and everybody else, and she would let you know that she prayed for you. She even brought our names up in her church so that the members and her bishop would pray for us as well. Sometimes when my mom would argue with me about something, I would always give her an answer back, and Mama Minnie would tell me never to answer her back. I tried, but it seemed that my mother was more disturbed by me and Grover staying with her. She had a mean streak in her, and once when I talked back, she picked up my iron baton that I marched with in the band and tried to hit me hard with it. I believed in respecting your elders back then, but knowing that this would have terribly injured me, I grabbed it and took it away from her.

It was so funny to me when she'd always give Grover the duty of snapping green beans for our dinner. He would do it so fast that one time we found string beans on the top of our garage. Grover would always find a way to get around doing what he didn't want to do. He tickled me so many times. Mr. Samuel occasionally bought me clothes, and one time he bought me a matching suit, hat, and shoes for Easter. I was so happy because I knew I would look so nice for Easter in church. But he asked me privately if I would give him a kiss for what he had bought. I said no though. I probably would have given him a kiss if he'd asked for it in the presence of my grandmother or mother. But this didn't feel right. I guess he was disappointed; however, I'd heard some of their bedtime arguments, and I thought maybe he wanted other people to show their appreciation for him. I joined the church on that

Easter Sunday, and I honestly don't know if I just wanted to show off my outfit or if I really wanted to join. My mother was so proud, and now we belonged to the same church. Sometime after that, I remember giving my life to God and depending on Him to show me the way. I was so glad that I had already joined the church. I asked the Lord to forgive me if I was just showing off on that Easter Sunday. When I was baptized at my church, I felt brand new, and I sensed that my sins had been washed away and that I was a new creature in God. I trusted God to save me. I did give my life over to Him. I started attending Sunday school, and I began teaching Sunday school classes along with one of my Norcom High School classmates.

Mr. Samuel did another thing for me that I'd never forget. He taught me how to drive. He used his fine vehicle, and he was patient too. I was glad that he wanted to do this for me. I was only fifteen, but on the paperwork I said I was sixteen. I did the required driving and parking, and then I got my driver's license.

There came a time when Mr. Samuel was forced to retire from the navy yard for some reason, although he didn't want to stop working. He couldn't find anything to do to take up those hours and years that he had worked, so he had a mental breakdown. I had married and was living in Northern Virginia when a neighbor called to tell me that he had moved all the furniture out of the house and left it on the lawn. He was hospitalized for a while, but my mother was so afraid of what he would do that she moved out of the house and got her own apartment. I never saw Mr. Samuel again. A friend of mine said that he lost his home and that she had seen him from time to time entering and leaving a motel room in Portsmouth. His brother in North Carolina came and moved Mr. Samuel with him until he eventually passed away. It's so wonderful that when we do become ill or dysfunctional, Jesus always puts someone in our path to help us. What a blessing! I feel sorry that his life's journey ended like this. All in all, I think he'd been a good man.

Chapter 5

G rover and I were sent to the proper schools in Portsmouth. I was in the eighth grade when I enrolled in I. C. Norcom High School.

Grover was in the sixth grade. I did very well while at Norcom. Some of my accomplishments made me realize that I emulated so much of my father's character, in addition to being well rounded and bright in the classroom. I was the head majorette of the marching band for four years, a charter member of the Agape Honor's Society, and a member of the 1958 homecoming court. I was voted the most popular senior girl in my graduating class. Since I was an outstanding student, I was selected to be an I. C. Norcom debutante by the Eurekas, a men's organization who selected our school's debutantes. My friend Alveria and I were first overlooked in the selection, but a staff member saw to it that we were included in the selections. We were honor roll students, and many felt that we were worthy of being debutantes. In 1958, the Alpha Kappa Alpha ladies were not selecting debutantes at the time. I also had graduated third in the 1958 graduating class of more than two hundred students. For my excellence in academic achievement, I received a scholarship to Norfolk State University in Norfolk, Virginia. I had to fight for a scholarship there though. I had been unintentionally omitted as the third honor graduate, and I would not have gotten the scholarship, which was traditionally offered to the top three graduates, had I not taken it upon myself to write a professor at Norfolk State University and let him know of this omission. That professor, whom I knew from church, went over to Norcom, told the administrators of my dilemma, and had them research the graduation records. I now encourage all students to keep a record of their accomplishments and averages themselves, as sometimes errors unintentionally occur with administrators. After all, they have so many records to keep up with. To my relief, the administrators did admit that this had been an unintentional oversight. I was the third honor graduate, and the professor came to my home in Portsmouth with this newfound information and the scholarship offer. *Thank God!* My mom did domestic work at that time, and she had told me that she could not afford to send me to college. But as God would have it, now I was college-bound with a scholarship to cover my tuition.

Grover, however, was charming, and he had a beautiful smile. But he was not interested in his junior high school subjects as much as he was interested in having nice clothes, which neither of us had at that time. Like most kids, he wanted to fit in with the other students and wear nice things. The whole time I was at Norcom, my mom outfitted me mainly in one of her friend's hand-me-down clothes, or if I had to be onstage at school for any reason, I borrowed clothes from my friends. Grover was proud to let others know that his sister was the well-liked head majorette they saw prancing behind the drum major, Lee Ward, in Portsmouth parades. I loved Grover immensely, and he loved me. He got in trouble a couple of times. My maternal grandmother (Mama Minnie), a sincerely devout Christian, went to court and begged officials to release Grover, and they did.

Chapter 6

Grover moved to New York without finishing school and started a new life. In New York, he married, and he and his wife had two children—a girl and a boy. His girl, Latarsha Burthey, has many of my qualities, and Timothy Burthey, has many qualities of his father and his uncle Rember. Latarsha is independent and strong, and I know she will continue to move upward and onward whether she has help from anyone else or not. She has proven this to us in so many ways. She had the determination to make it on her own. His son, Timothy, loves to research the ancestry of the Burthey family and is proud to be a Burthey. He investigates anyone with the Burthey surname. He is very intelligent, and he is so much like his uncle Rember, who had a terrific mind. I do love my niece and nephew.

My brother Rember Jr. had one daughter, Tracey Britton, from Atlantic City, New Jersey, and yes, we love her too. She is strong-willed, and she sets and vocalizes her goals. She is also a good planner, and she loves children. I have known her to be a very independent person, which is good since she's now lost both her father and mother. Prior to the movie *Roots* coming out, Tracey said she did not know who her father was. But she was so impressed by the movie that she decided to trace her roots after getting some information from her mom. Rember had worked during the summer in Atlantic City, which is how he had met and courted her mom. Tracey discovered who her father was and where he lived. She called the funeral home in Durham and talked with one of my aunts about her dilemma in trying to locate her father. She left a message and asked Rember to call her.

Rember also has children from his first marriage. I have fond thoughts of all my nephews and nieces. These young people are doing what they want in life, and they serve as wonderful role models for children and others in our family and in other families as well.

Chapter 7

I often think of the success stories of my nieces and nephews when I read the poem by Maya Angelou "And Still I Rise." They serve as unique, wonderful examples that we can rise from any mistakes or negative situations in which we may find ourselves, no matter how bad they may seem at the time. I have so much respect for them overcoming the odds and rising to the top.

My brother Grover had an unfortunate accident in New York and died. This broke my heart as I loved him so much. I was in the hospital with postpartum depression, which happened after the birth of my son and before Grover's death. He was on his way to see me at the hospital, but he passed away before he left New York. I was unable to go to his funeral because I was in the hospital. I regret to this day that we never were able to say goodbye to each other. I looked up one of his sons when I was in Portsmouth on sorority business once. He was so happy when he learned that I was his aunt. He said he always figured he had other family. He visited me two or three times at my home in Fort Washington, Maryland. We were all so happy that he was able to bond with his sister and brother, Latarsha and Timothy, who lived in New York at the time. Latarsha and Timothy welcomed him into the family. Unfortunately, he was returning from a visit in New York to see them when he was killed in an automobile accident. The devil is so busy! But God gave him a satisfied mind before he died because he had finally met his other family members.

Chapter 8

At Norfolk State University, I majored in business education. As an education major, I received another scholarship for education students that the university would pay back after each year I taught in Virginia.

My dad contacted me by letter at my mom's address, and he asked me to send him some bedroom shoes. I let my mom know because I had no money to do that for him, and she sent him the shoes. During my first year at Norfolk State, my father died of pneumonia in the hospital facility. My uncles had the body. All three of us kids went to the funeral service, and Mildred (his wife and our stepmother) actually came. We kids didn't know what to say to her. Our relationship was strained. But all of us got through the funeral. I remember putting my hand on my dad's forehead when I was alone with his body at the funeral home to ensure that he had actually passed on. He was ice cold. It gave me closure when I did this and attended his funeral. I was then ready to return to Norfolk State and complete my college work.

Chapter 9

During my matriculation at Norfolk State University, I never had to pay tuition or pay for textbooks. God made a way for me to complete college. In my sophomore year, I got pregnant by my high school boyfriend, Cleveland Crudup, who had also attended Norfolk State but who was now attending Virginia Union University in Richmond, Virginia. Although he lived in Norfolk, his parents wanted to keep us apart by sending him to Virginia Union University so that he could complete college. He never did though. His mother and grandmother arranged for me to have an abortion by a doctor in our area. I wanted to finish school, so I went along with the abortion while still attending Norfolk State. My mother could see that I was pregnant, but she didn't talk much about the pregnancy. I remember the Thursday before I had the abortion, the doctor pushed a coat hanger up in me and said the abortion would happen over the weekend. It did. It was a boy. When I went to the bathroom on Friday morning, the fetus dropped into the toilet. I had a bittersweet feeling. I was told by the Crudups that I should wrap the fetus in newspaper and that the mother and grandmother would be by to get it. They came and got the *package* and said they burned it in the incinerator of their restaurant. This whole procedure was devilish and unfortunate. My baby died, and I could have died; however, God had me. That Saturday, I had an accounting class, and I went right to it that day as if nothing had happened. I couldn't stand thinking about the abortion that had killed my baby boy, but now I could finish college on time. Since I had been showing, I figured everyone knew what had happened, but no one said a word to me about it. With belief, you only have to pray to God for the forgiveness of your sins and repent. I have prayed, intermittingly, throughout my lifetime for God to forgive me for being a participant in the abortion of my son. In my junior year of college, my high school sweetheart and I were married in a church wedding. He had been the love of my life.

The one who had given me the abortion attended the wedding. He did the work of the devil to me and other girls. He was a murderer. I wanted to graduate with my class. He, too, wanted me to complete college though. I'm reminded that I attended Norfolk State from 1958 to 1962. These were Jim Crow years in our country, and Negroes could not eat at the lunch counters at one of the department stores in the downtown Norfolk area. About twenty to twenty-five Norfolk Staters, including me, tried to integrate the lunch counters there. We walked from the university to the store downtown and stood at the counters because we were not allowed to sit there. The store employees began removing the seats at the counters so we could not sit down.

For about two months, we continued to march downtown and stand at the counters. Finally, the store took off the seats and put oil around the area where the seats used to be, so that if we stood there we would get oil on our clothing. We began to dress accordingly. Getting oil on our clothing did not deter us. In about four months, the store put the seats back in place because they were losing money from the Caucasians who could not sit there either. Now when I visit the store in downtown Norfolk, the food counters are open to all. I always think about our student movement and what we had to do to integrate the lunch counters. I feel proud that we protested peacefully with positive results. Many of today's millennials have no idea about what was done to integrate a restaurant, lunch facilities, and other places so all could eat there. They take for granted that they can eat anywhere they like and that things have always been this way.

Chapter *10*

S till moving forward in school, I maintained the highest academic average in the university's junior class. Again, I had to fight to be recognized for my educational accomplishment because someone else had been named as the one with the highest average in the junior class, and given this prestigious award for doing so. One of my male friends always kept up with my averages and accomplishments. He was like my protector. He told me that I had the highest average in the junior class. We went to the university administrators together with this, and sure enough, they acknowledged that mine was the highest. So they had to give me an award. The other person had already gotten one. In 1962, my senior year, I was elected by the faculty to appear in the book *Who's Who in American Colleges and Universities.* As God would have it, I continued to excel, and in the university's 1962 graduating class, I was named salutatorian in the class of more than four hundred graduates. The valedictorian's academic average was 3.99, and mine was 3.98. Still, I had no semblance of the painful knowledge that mental illness would influence my life after marrying and bringing an adorable son into this world.

Mrs. Clarine Roberts of Portsmouth, my high school business teacher, had followed my progress in college, and she felt I was worthy to be a member of her sorority, Alpha Kappa Alpha Sorority, Inc. She voluntarily sponsored me, and I was initiated in 1962 by Portsmouth's Gamma Delta Omega chapter. Then I became a member of the Alpha Kappa Alpha Sorority, Inc. I returned to Northern Virginia and joined the Arlington/Alexandria Zeta Chi Omega chapter of Alpha Kappa Alpha Sorority, Inc., in January 1963. This has been my only chapter affiliation. I am currently a Golden soror. You become a Golden soror when you have been a member of the sorority for fifty years. I have now almost fifty-six years of membership.

Chapter *11*

Upon graduation from the university, my husband and I journeyed to Northern Virginia so I could accept a job offer at Luther Jackson High School in Fairfax County, teaching high school students typewriting and other business courses. My husband was still in the job market. His first job was at the embassy of India in Washington, DC, as a messenger. He was well liked there, and we were invited to all the embassy's after-five parties. Little did we know that the devil was happy for our move because he had plans to interfere with my success and happiness with my husband at that time.

I loved my first teaching position at Luther Jackson in Merrifield, Virginia, and I really enjoyed the closeness I had with my students. Many of them stated that I was their favorite teacher. I required much of them, and they worked hard to meet my goals and please me. I taught along with another new business education teacher by the name of Rosslyn Short, who was from Virginia. Since we were young and just out of college and close to their ages, the students seemed to love us more. We served as role models for them on how you could be successful and even teach others if you were focused and diligent in your academic achievements. Rosslyn was married to an army general from Portsmouth, who was also a graduate of I. C. Norcom High School. Rosslyn taught at Luther Jackson for only a year, and then she went to Arizona to join her husband, who was stationed there. That left me as the only black business education teacher in Fairfax County Public Schools. I didn't like going to countywide business education meetings for this reason. After about five years, the Fairfax County Public Schools were integrated, and I was assigned to Thomas Jefferson Senior High School, in that county, as a business education instructor.

Chapter *12*

Meanwhile, my husband was hanging out at different clubs almost every night. He said that this was because he had never been out of Norfolk to live before, and he was excited by DC and its nightlife. Well, being a teacher, I could not hang out with him. I had to grade papers, keep up on my lesson planning, and be fresh and rested to begin each day with my students. I didn't like him hanging out like that, so I was quite unhappy with him doing so. The devil was happy. You see, while I was interested in church and having a successful teaching career, the devil had his hooks in him at that time. He would take me out occasionally with him to meet some of his friends, and we began to go to a restaurant in DC, called Wings and Things, at the end of the evening before going home. Norfolk State alumni had a chapter in DC, and they would have cabarets often, so we would usually attend with friends. Right about this time when I was teaching at Thomas Jefferson Senior High School, I started to beg my husband and tell him that we should start a family and have a baby. This was about five years into our marriage. He was an only child, and he was against this idea. He always said that babies and children were only trouble, and I knew he didn't want any children. But I talked him into it and managed to get pregnant anyway. He began staying out more after work. I always had dinner prepared for him, and it was disappointing that he wouldn't even call me and let me know he wasn't coming home. I felt an emotional loneliness that I had never felt before. This situation worried me so much, and without realizing it, I began a slow, torturous descent into depression. I tried as hard as I could not to feel upset because I knew emotional pain might cause harm to my baby. However, I used to cry and write him notes and leave them on the table for him to read. For a time, this was our only means of communication.

I went into labor two days after Christmas in 1966. My baby, Darrin Cleveland Crudup, was born on December 27, 1966. To me, giving birth was the most physically painful thing I had ever endured in my life. I had never had any type of pain or discomfort during my menstrual periods, although many of my friends told me how they suffered cramps and became so sick that they couldn't go to school, or had to go to bed during their periods. When my obstetrician finally came to the hospital, she said she was going to do an epidural. I lost consciousness as I kept saying to her, "Hurry! Hurry! Hurry!" When I was conscious again, I remember the nurse bringing this cute little baby to me. His thick hair was tied up with a blue ribbon. He was so adorable! The nurse approached my bed to hand me the baby, but I must have made an ugly, distorted face because she backed away from my bed and did not hand me my baby at that time. When I was wheeled out of the room past my husband, I told him, "I don't *ever* want to go through this again." And I never had a baby again. Darrin is my only child. But God blessed me with a sweet and handsome grandson in 2017, who's like my second child.

Chapter *13*

The next thing I knew after giving birth, I woke up in some other hospital in the psychiatric division. I had no idea what had happened to me. The doctors said I had suffered from postpartum depression. I guessed that postpartum depression shows up after the baby is born. In my opinion, it had come from all the strong emotional feelings and anxieties that I had felt before giving birth. Others have had it, and your children, grandchildren, or great-great-grands may have it in the future. One never knows!

When I didn't come home from the hospital with my baby, my mother came to the hospital to see me. But she didn't like what she saw because I was really out of it. Once, I was just stuffing my food in my mouth as fast as I could because I was overcome with the sensation of hunger. I know this must have looked crazy to her and anybody else! Looking back, now I know that I was diabetic then. I suffered from diabetes even in high school where my professors tried to help me with my shakiness and nervousness when I'd try to present a project in front of my classmates. One English professor even brought in a recorder to tape my presentations and show me that a lot of the nervousness was just inside my head. At these times, my glucose levels would drop so low that I felt so very shaky, weak, and hungry. My mom had never seen me carry on like that. She left my home in Arlington, Virginia, and went back to Portsmouth to be with her mother and Mr. Samuel. My mental instability surprised her just as it had surprised me. This problem had never flared up while I was living with her or when I had achieved so much success in school. My husband said my mom couldn't stand the idea that I wasn't doing well after having my baby. My husband had to drive our baby down to Norfolk, Virginia, to his mother, Mrs. Otelia Crudup, who cared for him until I got out of the hospital. At that time, none of my doctors had shared with me the fact that I was diabetic, even though they had run so many blood tests and should have known this. Dr. Henderson, whom I would later meet, should have definitely known from all the blood tests he had ordered after I was admitted to the hospital so many times. But he seemed rather secretive to me. I guess he mainly addressed the mental stress and depression issues, and I must say he did an excellent job at that. He never mentioned diabetes to me. So many years of my adult life, I had never been treated for diabetes, which accounted for the shaky and spastic way I would feel sometimes, especially when my glucose levels dropped. It is a common thread in my family's health history. My paternal grandmother, my brother, my first cousin, and I'm sure many other family members had died from diabetes and heart disease. Years later, after I was working in my second career, I was eventually diagnosed as being a diabetic. I took classes on managing diabetes at Southern Maryland Hospital in Clinton, Maryland, to become educated about the causes, care, and precautions needed for one to live a healthy life and keep diabetes in check.

During this first hospitalization, I was a mental case by then. I suffered with postpartum depression and diabetic problems, and I had to talk to the psychiatrist on a regular basis. I was so bad off that the doctor decided that I might return to normalcy if he did electric shock treatment on me. He put two instruments on my head—one on each side—and then it felt like I took my last breath and died. But the devil is a liar. I woke up. I did not die. I stayed in the hospital for a while longer. My husband visited me often. Once, he said he wanted to make love to me so badly, and no one was in the room with us. He closed the door to my room, got in the bed with me, and had intercourse with me. He seemed sex crazed like that, even at home. I told one of the nurses about it, and she said that he was insane for doing that in a hospital.

After a while, the doctor said that I could leave the hospital, and he referred me to another psychiatrist named Dr. Arthur R. Henderson. Dr. Henderson was one of the best psychiatrists in his field. He was a godsend for me for many years.

Before seeing Dr. Henderson, my husband thought it would be a good thing for us to go on a trip to Luray Caverns when I was released from the first hospital. We went to Luray Caverns, and for the entire time we drove up and around mountains and curves, I thought my husband was going to kill me. That was my state of mind at the time. I felt so embarrassed that this happened to me and that all my neighbors and friends would know that this had happened to me. They told me, "You will be all right. We've heard of postpartum depression before." They were very sympathetic.

Chapter *14*

I was able to continue teaching after having my baby—this time at two different junior high schools in another county. I worked so hard at my new junior high schools that the tension and stress of teaching started taking its toll on me, and I was hospitalized many times under Dr. Henderson's care. One of my principals suggested that I retire on disability. But as God would have it, I acquired a teaching job at a high school in Arlington. Being at one school was certainly better than being assigned to two schools. I enjoyed teaching high school students more than the junior high students, who were so playful and mean to one another and fought a lot. A teaching coworker at one of the junior high schools was very depressed about the way students were misbehaving in class, and they were so mean to my coworker that he eventually made the ultimate sacrifice. He took his own life. I believe that he really needed to talk to a doctor like I did and get help in coping with his feelings and with the depression and problems with the kids. I would advise anyone who suffers from depression to talk to a therapist, namely a psychiatrist, who can prescribe medication to help you feel better about yourself and the other problems that life sometimes brings. When I think of him, I know I did the right thing in seeking out the care of a professionally trained person like Dr. Henderson.

The Lord looked out for me when I was offered a job at the high school. One day the word got out in the faculty lounge, where I worked, about what that teacher had done. I knew his situation and how it had tormented him, and I was truly sorry that he felt this was his only way out. I didn't make any comments about him to the faculty, though.

Chapter 15

Meanwhile, the relationship between my husband and me had gotten worse since I'd had my baby. He seemed jealous of his own son, and he said that since the baby's birth, I didn't have time to spend with him. I was always doing something for the baby. I tried to reason with him by saying that if he helped me with the baby, I'd have more time to do things with him. Instead he started spending more time away from home and in the streets, drinking and partying. I even asked one of my sorors named Mrs. Evelyn Syphax, the Zeta Chi Omega chapter's founder, to keep Darrin for me. She said she would, and I took him to her. In a day or two, Cleveland had insisted that I tell him where Darrin was. He went around Soror Syphax's house and told her that I was ill and that he wanted his son back. She gave him Darrin along with an apology, saying she didn't know I was ill. She did me another big favor and accepted my son into her school. It was a Montessori school. Her staff potty-trained him at her school too. She did all she could to help me with him. I was so very grateful that God had put her in my path. She asked me on other occasions if there was anything she could do for me. She was such a giving soul, and I was indeed blessed and glad that she was my sorority sister and so very concerned about me. I was happy that she was a part of my life's journey. She's now deceased.

Chapter *16*

I couldn't depend on Cleveland to come home with our car so that I'd have transportation to make my hair and other appointments I needed to keep myself up as a professional teacher. However, I had a good friend who knew us well and lived close to us. She knew my situation and let me use her car on Saturdays when I had hair appointments. Most of the time, Cleveland was never there when I needed him. He started staying out the entire weekend instead of just one night. Once, when he was asleep at home, I looked in his pockets. He had a little book and napkins with the names and phone numbers of sixteen women. I wrote in the book, "Go on to #17," and put it back in his pocket. He realized what I had done in a few days and swore to me that these were just friends he'd met, not girlfriends. He even started leaving me home on weekends and driving to Norfolk—or so he said—to visit his mother and grandmother.

One weekend when he returned from Norfolk, he found that I had bought my own car. He was surprised and said, "You don't know anything about taking care of a car." But I had learned a lot from people who did know about cars, and now I had needed transportation. God was so good for providing and helping me figure things out.

Chapter 17

One weekend we went to a party. We took our son so he could sleep while we were there. When the party was over and everyone except us had left, I kept telling him that we should leave because I wanted to take Darrin to church the next day. Plus, the host and hostess had church plans as well. Cleveland became so angry with me because he didn't want to go home. The party hostess said, "Well, if it's time to go, it's time to go." Finally, he went into the bedroom and got our baby. When we arrived home, he was still angry—so much so that he pointed a gun at me. I prayed very hard to God and promised Him that if He'd let me live through the night, I would leave my husband. I worried about him since he finally left the house again and had consumed so much alcohol. Let's face it. I've been a real worrier in my lifetime. But since I've learned to depend on Jesus, I don't worry like that anymore. I just ask God to intercede and help me make good decisions in solving problems. And God works things out magnificently.

Chapter *18*

One time when we were dating, Cleveland had drawn a gun on his own father. Back then, he had worked at his dad's service station all summer with hopes of coming to pick me up from my great-aunt Martha King's home in Manhattan. Aunt Martha was my paternal grandmother, Mama Susie's sister, and she treated me like I was her daughter. She didn't have any children. Since high school and all through college, I had spent my summers with her. She was a seamstress, and she would make me dresses and sometimes a complete wardrobe of clothes for high school and college so that I'd be able to look nice in school. She appreciated the fact that I did well in school and that I was trying to succeed in life. She took me to see many sites in New York City, including Broadway, Macy's, Radio City Music Hall, Coney Island, and many other places. She was a travel agent for her church, and I traveled with her many times. She taught me about having fun with slot machines at casinos, mostly in Las Vegas and Atlantic City, and she allowed me to enjoy cruises with her. We went on about seven or eight cruises together and with her friends. I still enjoy the casino slots, and although it's considered gambling, I feel it's playing games with a machine, not hard-core gambling. I'd never seen anything in the Bible about gambling. I know it's not in God's plan though. I really need help with this. Aunt Martha knew my dad was deceased now, and my mom couldn't afford to help. So she was very generous with helping me. She would send me money whenever I needed it for school stuff, bills, and household items after I was divorced. She helped me make payments on the sauna that I still own. *Won't God provide?* I thought. Her husband, Uncle Cliff, always treated me well, and he also said that I was Aunt Martha's favorite niece. His kindness receded once, and I grew afraid of him. Aunt Martha wasn't home, and he came up to me and put his arms around me and asked me to give him a kiss. I had no desire to do this, so I didn't. I just said, "No, get away from me!" I really hated to have to tell my aunt about this incident, but I felt that if I didn't, he would continue to make advances at me. I'd never feel comfortable around him again. So when Martha returned home, I told her what he had done. Well, she got on him about this, and of course, he denied that it had ever happened. He said, "This kid is lying, and I want her out of this apartment."

Martha believed me and said that I didn't have to go anywhere. This was really a bad situation, so I told Martha that I'd asked one of my girlfriends, Vannie, if I could spend the rest of the summer with her. She had let her sister Doris and our friend from college, Jean, stay with her before too. The three of us girls were working in New York for the summer. I told Vannie that I would pay her if she'd let me stay, and she agreed. Martha and I remained on good terms, and she wasn't surprised by what Uncle Cliff had done; however, she was angry as hell. She told some of our family members about it, and my cousins came around Vannie's place to make sure I was all right.

They laughed at Cliff and said that he couldn't stand the pressure being around me. They believed he had done just what I had said he had done. I was a college student at this time. I made arrangements for Cleveland to pick me up at the end of the summer that time; however, his dad said he hadn't done a good job for him that summer at the service station, and therefore he couldn't go to New York. Cleveland was upset and ended up pointing a gun at his dad. He just threatened him though. Knowing that this had happened, I worried that one day he might point one at me or Darrin. It seemed that God wanted me to make that move.

The night when he left our house after having too much alcohol, I made plans to leave him. He was missing from home too, and I was shaking all night. The next day I was emotionally wrecked. I called the police to report him missing. They told me that the person had to be missing at least twenty-four hours for the authorities to get involved. When they did get involved, I gave them one of his friend's telephone numbers, and they told me later that he was at that friend's house "sleeping it off."

Chapter *19*

I continued my work as a teacher as I made plans to leave him. I bought a sofa and stored it at a friend's home. I decided to leave him the Magnavox stereo that we had since he liked music so much, but I also determined that I would take our television for my son. I decided to leave one weekend when he had gone to Norfolk. I made arrangements to take Darrin to New York to a relative's home, and she was to keep him until I returned to pick him up. I contacted a student who had said that he and his uncle would come to move me out when I called. Before going to New York, I'd packed our clothes and left them in our laundry room downstairs in our apartment building.

With plans in place, I did leave him, and I moved to an apartment in Shirlington, a section of Arlington. I had already paid the first month's rent there. Everything worked out, and I was out of there! *Thank God!* When he returned from Norfolk, my son and I were not there. We were in our new apartment.

After we had been separated for a year without cohabitation, I was granted my divorce.

Cleveland was bitter through it all. The year after our divorce, he married again. I wasn't bothered or jealous about this, but I was so very grateful and relieved that my son and I didn't have to live with him, his jealousy, and his gun threats anymore.

Chapter *20*

Well, it was obvious, I'd learned through counseling, that I had picked up a tendency toward mental illness from my father. I was in and out of hospitals under Dr. Henderson's care so many times while I continued to teach. Sometimes I would telephone Dr. Henderson from work and ask him to admit me to the hospital because I wasn't thinking or feeling right. He would say, "Okay. I'll get you a bed." He never wanted to take a chance that I would do something *sick* at work. My appointments with him every three weeks and my necessary hospitalizations continued for as long as I worked. It was as if I'd been knocked down so many times, but because of God's grace and goodness as well as Dr. Henderson's expert care, I could pick myself up, brush myself off, and continue working through the next days, weeks, or months. I really came up on the rough side of the mountain. I thanked God for blessing Dr. Henderson with the knowledge and intelligence necessary to be one of the strong, supportive links I had at my command to help me overcome the downfalls in my life. Many people with mental instabilities are not as blessed as I was. Just read today's news about the suicides and murders by those with mental problems.

Chapter *21*

As my son grew older and started playing football, his dad began coming out to his practices. He didn't show any interest in him before when he was younger, but now he was showing an interest in his sports activities. I thought that he had plans to somehow get Darrin to live with him again.

One weekend when he was supposed to pick Darrin up for a visit with him, he came to my home and said, "I hear you're not sleeping too well." He'd heard this information from my brother, Rember Jr., who had separated from his family and moved to Maryland. He talked to me on the phone sometimes and would pass information about me to Cleveland. Of course, he'd tell me about Cleveland as well. He was the one who told me how bitter Cleveland was when I left him. Rember was jealous that Aunt Martha was helping me so much and that I cared so much for her. It didn't matter that the aunt he loved, and thought I should like, I never talked about. So, he assumed that it was because that aunt was not as financially blessed as Martha had been, although she'd never shown any interest in me. But Rember Jr., my own brother, thought that I liked Martha because of money. I sensed that he sided with Cleveland on everything since our divorce.

One weekend I was in bed when Cleveland came by for Darrin. He came into my room and said, "I hear that you're not sleeping so well. Take this pill. It will help you to sleep." Well, God has blessed me with the gift of intuition throughout the years. I knew something was up with that. He said, "Open your mouth." Then he dropped the pill in my mouth and said, "Swallow it." If he wasn't up to something, he would have stood over me to ensure that I had swallowed the pill. But instead he had rushed into my bathroom, checking my medications and probably putting more of those pills in one of the bottles. As soon as he rushed out of my room, I took the pill out of my mouth and hid it in my bed. I thought, *He must be nuts if he thinks I'm going to take a pill just because he said so.* He came back in the room and asked me if I had swallowed it. I said I had. Then he said, "Lift up your tongue." I did that, and he said, "Sleep well, Clarice. Sleep well."

Then he left the house with my son. I got right on the phone and called Dr. Henderson and told him what Cleveland had done, and Dr. Henderson told me to come back to the hospital and to bring the pill with me. I did this right away. He later told me that it would have killed me. He didn't tell me exactly what it was though. He called Cleveland and had him come in, and he told him that he knew he had tried to kill me. He told that man that the only reason he wouldn't tell the police about this was that he didn't want my son to have to be without a father for the rest of his life. After that, I often wondered who had given him the pill. I guess I'll never know. But the important thing was that God kept me alive. My intuition told me that Cleveland was giving me poison or something in that pill. He'd tried to get rid of me so he could raise his son from then on. He didn't want anything to do with Darrin in his younger years. Oh, how the devil had taken over his heart.

Chapter 22

God has always blessed me with nice cars. I've had two Corvettes and three or four Mercedes. I had totaled the red and silver Corvettes that I had. In an accident with one of them, I should have died. I'd decided that I was going to drive to New York to see one of my boyfriends, my third cousin Henry Gregg, whom I had fallen in love with when I had visited Aunt Martha in the summers before my high school years. Henry was allowed to go on some of our trips to Coney Island. Our love life had been put on hold during my marriage, but it had started up again after my divorce. I had the directions to New York in mind, but somehow from my home in Alexandria, I got completely lost in Washington, DC. I was afraid to stop and ask someone the directions to Interstate 95. I was driving around and around for so long that I became weary and defeated. I stepped on the gas as hard as I could then. I gave up and floored the gas pedal of the car and drove into a pole at a suicidal rate. The devil wanted me to commit suicide. The car was totaled. Fortunately, material things can be replaced. A crowd grew around me in the car. I stepped out of the car, unhurt, and I just stood there in a trance. Someone came up to me and said, "The police are going to come. Don't you think you should at least lie down on the ground? Is there someone we should call at home?" It sounded like a good idea to me, so I lay down on the ground, pretending to be hurt. I wasn't actually hurt. (God's miraculous power had saved me.) I guess the police got my ID, and somehow I ended up in the hospital with Dr. Henderson. I had left my son at home and given him my American Express card. I told him that if he needed anything, he could use the card. He said, "Okay, Mom. If you want to go to New York, just go ahead. I'll be all right." What a big boy! God knew that leaving my son alone was wrong and the work of the devil. He knew that my son needed his mother. The police had called my home, and my son gave them his uncle Rember's phone number. Rember told them to take me to Dr. Arthur Henderson at Providence Hospital. Either Rember or Cleveland went to my home and picked up Darrin. One of them kept him until I was well again. In the meantime, Rember went to the scene of the accident and took pictures of the car. He told me later that there was a small amount of my blood on the dashboard. He didn't think I would make it from just looking at the totaled vehicle.

Chapter *23*

I had another brush with death when I was young and foolish and had tried marijuana once with a friend of Henry's in New York. I became nauseous and started shaking uncontrollably. The friend had me drink Coca-Cola right away and continue sipping soda for the rest of the evening. She told me later that this had been a bad batch of marijuana, but I recuperated after drinking the soda. I'd had another brush with death. I vowed that I'd never use marijuana again, and I haven't. Since that time, Henry, a diabetic who drank and did anything else he wanted to do, had serious problems with diabetes and had to have a leg amputated. He went to a long-term care facility, where he eventually died. I know that I'm a child of God. He kept saving me over and over. He has plans for my life. If it hadn't been for God, I wouldn't be living right now.

Chapter 24

When I returned to my high school position, some of the female teachers were talking in the lounge. They said I kept getting new cars because I had sugar daddies. This was not true. Too many people look at others and try to judge them. We are supposed to leave the judging to God. Gossip can bring bad reputations. You can't believe everything you hear. I've had God's grace and blessings on my life. Because I looked good and God helped me afford fancy cars, many thought I was a prostitute. This was not true. I had never been a prostitute and didn't need to be one to pay my bills. God made a way for me. He had even put Aunt Martha in my life to help me financially. I was also a great accountant, and I knew how to budget my money so that I could buy whatever I wanted and could afford. I could figure out financial problems in my head. It also helped that in school I had discovered that I was blessed with a photographic memory for numbers. That's why you shouldn't try to judge others. You don't know what they've been through in their lives. You don't know what they are going through at any point in time.

Chapter 25

At the high school where I was employed, a group of us teachers started having lunch together, and if one had a birthday, we would buy the person a cake or do something special for the individual at lunchtime. My mom was terminally ill with cancer of the uterus. Her boyfriend Tommy, whom she dated after she and Mr. Samuel had separated, called my brother Rember and told him that Mom was sick. He said that if we wanted to see her alive again, we should come see her now. I took Darrin down on a Greyhound bus to see her as Rember didn't want to go down at that time. Tommy picked us up at the bus terminal and took us to our Mom's house. She was very ill, but she knew us. She had severe bedsores, and I felt like no one could do anything for her or even make her comfortable. She was glad to see Darrin, her grandson. I told her that I loved her, and she said, "I love you too." She was so bad off that I knew I never wanted to see her in that condition again. It was just so unbearable to see her that way. When we left her, I knew I'd never see her alive again. But I prayed that God would intercede and take her away from her misery. Tommy called me and asked me my birth date as well as the birth dates of my siblings. I provided this information. When I went back to work, Tommy called to say that Mom had passed on January 31, my birthday. I thought then that he and the funeral director had agreed that for some reason she should be taken out of her misery on my birthday. That day at school, I was on my way to meet the teachers I had lunch with to give them the sad news. I saw one of them in the hallway with my birthday cake, and I told her that my mother had passed that day. They felt badly for me. I assumed they shared my cake.

Rember called me and said he would be coming to drive us to the funeral in Portsmouth. Now every birthday I have, I remember that she passed on the same day. I feel that Tommy chose my birthday because she and I loved each other so. Rember didn't show any love for her, and he wasn't even on speaking terms with her before she passed. When we went to view her body though, he was silently crying. I thought maybe he felt guilty. He had been angry about her attending Grover's funeral and that she was seemingly so upset when our brother Grover died. He felt that she should not have even come to his funeral, but she did. Of course, I was in the hospital with postpartum depression and couldn't attend his funeral. My mom told me that Rember didn't speak to her at all at Grover's funeral. He was known to carry grudges against family members.

After my mom's funeral, Tommy took me to the bank to collect the small amount that she had left to me, and then he told me to pay for the gas he'd used driving me around. Of course, Rember was angry that she didn't leave him one cent. Mama Minnie was alive during that time. She informed me about a month later that Tommy had married my mother's neighbor who lived across the hall from her a few weeks after my mom had passed. The entire time Mom was sick, they'd been seeing each other. Later when I went down to visit Mama Minnie, she shared with me that Tommy had been chasing her—my ninety-year-old grandmother—around her house for sex. I would always wonder whether he ever sexually abused her. I never asked her about this. He was also married to my mom's former neighbor at the time he was chasing my grandmother around. I went to Mama Minnie's house one time that she had gone out of town to a church in North Carolina. She knew that I wanted to see her, and she told me that she had left her door key with my uncle so I could get it and stay at her house until she returned on Sunday night. Ironically, Tommy entered her house with a key. I was in bed, and he had the nerve to come in Mama Minnie's room and get in the bed with me. I slid out of the bed and said I would sleep in the living room. He knew he had done the wrong thing. He insisted that he would sleep in the living room, and he did. I slept in my grandmother's room. Even before this happened, it was evident that he was a very sick man. I told all this to Mama Minnie when she returned from North Carolina. Evidently, Tommy had the ungodly thought that he could have any woman regardless of age. It sickened me to know that he had chased my elderly grandmother around, and then he had thought that he could have me. I never inquired about him again. Forgive me, Lord, but I didn't pray for him. I really should have.

Chapter 26

After twenty years of teaching, being hospitalized, and seeing Dr. Henderson, I had a talk with the principal of the high school where I was working. He suggested that I retire from teaching on disability, and that's exactly what I did in 1982. However, I knew that God had chosen me for the teaching profession, and I genuinely loved working with young people. Even now I'm interested in what young people are doing and thinking and in helping them learn whenever I have the opportunity to do so. After I retired from teaching, I quickly became bored and started applying for jobs with the federal government within two months. I lived about five minutes from the gate at the Fort Belvoir army base, and I applied for jobs there too. Thank God I found a GS-3 clerk-typist position there. I should have applied for a higher GS position with all my experience, but at the time, I knew nothing about federal positions. After the clerk-typist position, I moved to a secretarial position, which was GS-5. Then I secured a GS-7/9/11 Department of Defense (DOD) accountant intern position. After completion of the DOD internship, I worked as an accountant at the Military District of Washington in Washington, DC, and Fort Belvoir's accounting and finance office on Fort Belvoir's army base for a total of ten years.

There were many other boyfriends, especially at the Fort Belvoir NCO Club, which I frequented. There were a number of ladies of the night who hung around in the military NCO clubs, but I wasn't one. However, I had the most trouble with the pimps who wanted me to turn tricks for them. I never did this because I had lots of pride in myself, my upbringing, and where I came from. I also thought it was wrong to misuse your vessel. I had never considered being a prostitute and never needed to. One of the pimps—I'd learned how to spot them—wanted me to feel like I needed him, and he felt defeated that I never did. I just liked to play bingo at the NCO club. Plus, I enjoyed the restaurants and liked playing cards with some of the patrons. After that, I was on my way home.

One of the sergeant majors, a friend of mine, warned me not to get involved with the pimp in any way because he would kill my s—. That's just the way he said it. He started the *S*, and I filled in the blank with *son*. One day after my son had gone to work at the Springfield Mall jewelry store, there was a loud *pop! pop! pop!* sound. Then my phone rang, and it was the pimp on the other end saying, "Now do you need me?" Then all of a sudden, he said, "Oh, goddamn!" and then he hung up. I quickly called my son to make sure he was all right. I told him that there had been some gunshots on the corner.

My son said, "Well, they'd better keep that shooting down on the corner, not where we live." Sure enough, some neighbors told me that someone had been shot in a car like my son's on the corner from us. I didn't see the pimp around for a long time, but I figured it out eventually. Someone was supposed to shoot my son, but the hit man shot at another car that looked like my son's. That person was the pimp, and the police had caught him as he was making the phone call to me. It was a year or so later when I spotted the pimp at a club. I recognized him, but he didn't recognize me with my new red hair and hairdo. I told my sergeant major friend that I'd seen him but that he hadn't seen me. I knew intuitively that I didn't want to deal in any way with a pimp. This one wanted so badly for me to need him that he would have killed my son to get to me. He served some time for his part in planning the hit on my son, and I haven't heard from him since. I knew that with his being an army man, he had gotten in some serious trouble. That was enough for me. Thank God for intuition and for manifesting his saving grace in my life!

Chapter 27

As a GS-11 accountant at Fort Belvoir, I audited the accounts there, and during an assignment I had been given by the top official at the finance and accounting office where I worked, I discovered some interesting findings. These findings were reported to the army base's commanding general there, and because of the nature of my work, she provided me with police protection wherever I went and arranged to have me transferred to the Audit Resolution Division of the US Department of Education in Washington, DC, with a promotion to GS-12, audit resolution specialist.

I later worked in the accounts receivable division as an accountant. From the accounts receivable division, I received a promotion to a GS-13 because I always provided quality work. As a GS-13, I worked in the student financial assistance division. The general from Fort Belvoir telephoned me at the Department of Education when I worked in audit resolution and asked if I was satisfied with my new position. She wanted to remove some of the people at Belvoir from their jobs because of fraudulent actions I reported in my work. I was satisfied, so she took corrective actions based on my findings while at Belvoir. God had made all this possible. Remember I had started working as a general service employee (GS-3).

Chapter 28

God began to show His power to me to make sure I continued to believe in and serve Him, especially when I would go to the hospital to rest.

Once when I had to wait for Dr. Henderson to arrive at the hospital, a nurse put me in a chair and secured my legs with chains so I couldn't move around. God showed me how to maneuver my feet to come out of the chains. The staff member in charge informed Dr. Henderson that I had gotten out of the chains, though she didn't know how. It was by God's power, not mine. Dr. Henderson told me not to feel special because I had gotten out of the chains. He said others had done that too. My intuition told me that he just didn't want me to think that I was special. But I knew I was special to God, and to God I gave—and continue to give—all the glory.

God made Himself evident to me almost every time I was in the hospital. Early on, when I was really sick, my father came into my room and told me everything was going to be all right. I told doctors about that, but I guess they didn't believe me. God began to show me His power in other ways as well.

Once, I was talking to Dr. Henderson and a nurse, and I pretended to pass out just to play with them. They both called out my name as loud as they could as I was falling. But I fell, and God sent me to another place. It was like a cave with large stones in it, and in it there were about eight old men with beards. It was like a holding place for them. They asked me, "How long are you going to keep us down here?" I didn't answer them because I didn't know what they were talking about. The next thing I knew, I was walking back into the room with Dr. Henderson and the nurse. Dr. Henderson didn't say a word to me. I sat on the floor, and the nurse came over to me and said, "Here's a blanket. I know you must be cold." I've never spoken to anyone about this incident.

I knew Dr. Henderson would tell me that I thought I was special but that I wasn't. I asked myself, "What happened to me? Did I die and come back? How did I get to that cave?" To this day, I don't have an answer, but I distinctly remember the cave with large rocks, the old men with beards, and what they asked me. Dr. Henderson did make a special call to my brother Rember, who was keeping my son at the time, and he asked him to bring my son in to see me. My son said to my brother, "It's Mom, and she's okay. She's okay!" Dr. Henderson was there and heard him make these statements.

Dr. Henderson told my son, "Yes, your mom is okay." I figured that Dr. Henderson had called them and told Rember to tell my son that something had happened to me.

My brother was surprised to see me too. There was more to come though. God would give me revelations and make miracles happen to show me His power whenever I was in the hospital. This is all true. I've remembered it all these years.

Chapter 29

Another miracle happened when I was in the hospital. Dr. Henderson was a witness to this, although he cannot tell anyone now because he passed away on July 9, 2005. Sometimes the patients in the psychiatric division of the hospital would go on little field trips or walks through the botanical gardens, or they would just walk as a group with the doctor or a staff member to get a break from being inside the hospital. Some of us patients were casually walking back to the hospital when all of a sudden, God lifted me up, and I started flying like a bird. I came down next to Dr. Henderson and said, "Hi, Dr. Henderson!"

He mumbled, "Hi, Clarice," because he had seen me flying. No, I wasn't hallucinating! What could he say?

One of the guys walking with us asked the other one, "Hey, man, did you see that?"

The other guy said, "Yeah, man. Damn!" We went back to the hospital, and Dr. Henderson took us into the room where the pool tables were. He sat down, and I went to the pool table. I'd never played pool in my life, but I took the long cue stick, hit the ball, and all four or five of the balls went into a different hole at the same time. I said, "Dr. Henderson, did you see that?"

He said, "Yeah, I saw you." I knew that was a hard feat to accomplish. But we didn't talk about that either. I was definitely having a good day!

Dr. Henderson assigned me to an evening group session. One evening at the end of our group meeting, he said in a matter-of-fact way, "Clarice, I want you to walk with me to a meeting next week. All you have to do is just walk behind me. It'll be a group of people in the room."

I asked, "Do I have to say anything?"

He said, "No, all you have to do is walk behind me. That's it."

So after group that next week, I went to the meeting with him and just walked behind him into the room. One person asked, "How do you feel walking behind Dr. Henderson?"

I just hunched up my shoulders and said, "Okay." There were a lot of people in the room looking at me (doctors, I think). It was obvious to me that they just wanted to see me for some reason. I didn't know why. As Dr. Henderson would say, I wasn't special, so why were they there? But truthfully, I believe that in God's sight, we're all unique and special. He made us that way.

Chapter 30

Well, after I was released from the hospital, I went back to work as usual. Rember passed away in 1993 from a massive heart attack, which was the same year that I moved to my final work location in the US Department of Education. I had spoken to him on the telephone the night before he died, and he had invited me to come to his house the next day for a cookout. When I arrived at his home, he was already dead. His wife said she knew he was dead before the paramedics left the house with him because he had turned purple. She and Rember had only been married for eight months when he passed. Although I had just begun working at the Department of Education, some of my new coworkers attended his funeral. I found this act to be very supportive, and I was impressed by them.

Chapter *31*

I was an accountant and financial management analyst at the US Department of Education in Washington, DC. After I had worked the additional ten years at the department, I retired from the federal government with twenty years of service—ten in DOD and ten at the Department of Education. I had retired from two careers now—teaching and accounting with the federal government. In all, I had worked forty years, counting the twenty years of teaching. I went back to the hospital for problems with depression once before retiring and once after retirement. Before retirement, I needed to release some of the pressure that I felt by having leave without pay issues held against me by my supervisor. Leave without pay can put one into bankruptcy. God is so very good though. One of my neighbors who lived two doors from me gave me a small loan to help me out a little. I had to get statements from my doctor at the time, Dr. Clarke, who was Dr. Henderson's substitute. He verified that I had entered the hospital in an emergency and that I couldn't request the sick leave ahead of time. This worked, and it was a blessing that I was able to work with human resources personnel at the Department of Education, and they helped me make my retirement happen.

After retirement I was just so bored that I felt I was losing it again. My son was working, and since he lived with me, I was home alone after I retired. I worked on puzzles, and my former mother-in-law gave me an organ to play. She also gave me a few lessons in crocheting. But none of this satisfied me. That's the reason I suffered another bout with depression and was hospitalized for a short time again. Fortunately, now I just see a doctor about once every three months to get medication to help me sleep and deal with the bipolar depression for which I'd been diagnosed. Nowadays I talk very little to this therapist as he's not a psychiatrist. He's a medications expert. The visits with him only last about ten minutes, which is all the time he needs to write prescriptions, as he keeps my bipolar depression issues in check.

Chapter *32*

After retirement with forty years of service—twenty with the state of Virginia and twenty with the federal government—I was extremely bored by not having to continue my work routine. I'm sure this is how Mr. Samuel felt when he was forced to retire. Neither of us had plans for what we would do after retirement. I believe that people should make plans of how they will use their time after they retire. Otherwise, in my opinion, boredom can take its toll on you.

When I was working for the federal government after I had been a teacher, some individuals asked me if that was "double dipping." It wasn't, though, because there is a clear separation of the state and federal governments.

Chapter 33

I began looking around for some volunteer opportunities or part-time work. I substituted at an elementary school a few streets over from me. Since I had only taught high school before, I found elementary school to be exhausting. The children showed up, acted out with each other, and showed no respect at all for substitute teachers. Many times regular teachers would have to come into the classroom, or I'd have to call the front office to get the students to settle down. They were so happy that their regular teacher wasn't there that day. I felt so sorry for the good students who wanted to learn and do the assignments that their regular teachers had left for them. I didn't like being a substitute teacher for elementary students at all. It was so bad that I joked to others that I had to drag myself home and rest on the sofa for at least an hour before doing anything else. I decided that retirement wasn't supposed to be like that. So I discontinued substituting. It wasn't for me.

I did become a Shaklee distributor for a few years, and I was actually successful. I had so many sales that shortly after becoming a distributor, I became a Shaklee corporation director less than a year after working for them. My friends assisted me by introducing their friends to Shaklee and using the products themselves. I still use some Shaklee products and still fill orders occasionally.

I stayed with Shaklee long enough to walk across the stage as a successful entrepreneur with Shaklee's organization in San Francisco. There were thousands of Shaklee users and distributors there, and it was very exciting being with them, knowing that Shaklee could compete with the top distributors of healthy products. But it has continued to be something that I work on occasionally along with other activities in my retirement. I continue to receive calls from clients who will use nothing else but Shaklee products for health, beauty, weight loss, washing, and cleaning chores.

Chapter 34

Retirement was not without its excitement. I had the opportunity to continue being active in a political sense. In 2009, our nation brought forward the first black president of the United States. His name was Barack Hussein Obama II. Mr. Obama was born on August 4, 1961, at the Kapoliana Medical Center for Women and Children in Honolulu, Hawaii. Proudly, I exercised my right to vote twice—once for him and his running mate, Joe Biden, during his first term and once for his second term. He made news throughout the world as he honorably served as president of the United States from January 20, 2009, to January 20, 2017. Mr. Joe Biden won as his vice president. President Obama was the forty-fourth president of the United States (POTUS). He was a member of the Democratic Party, and he had also completed Harvard Law School.

President Obama brought his family with him to grace the White House. Michelle Obama, the First Lady of the United States (FLOTUS), her mother, and her two daughters, Sasha and Malia, would now be considered the first family. Some questioned whether our first black president was indeed a citizen of the United States and asked that his birth certificate be carefully scrutinized. Yes, indeed, President Obama was a legal, bona fide citizen of the United States. Unlike some former presidents, neither President

Obama nor his family brought any scandals to the presidency. He made our nation and the world so proud of his accomplishments. The same can be said for his wife, Michelle, and their children. Michelle's main emphasis as the First Lady addressed children's obesity, and she showed them how to plant and care for gardens. She was one of the most charming and well-liked first ladies that we have had. She was very intelligent, and she was an attorney in her own right.

Neither can I forget the US Postal Service's tribute at a stamp event for Maya Angelou on April 7, 2016. How honored I was to have been invited to this event by the US Post Office on the first day that the Maya Angelou stamp was issued. I attended this event along with a favorite soror of mine named Margretta Tinsley. I had actually invited her to attend with me. This tribute to Maya Angelou was held at the Warner's Theater in Washington, DC. Oprah Winfrey graced the stage and gave a few comments on the honoree, Maya Angelou. It was a complete surprise when President Barack Obama came onstage to share in the stamp tribute, and on behalf of women, he asked that all members of Alpha Kappa Alpha Sorority stand. Well, here was our sorority sisters' opportunity to shine. I stood along with Soror Margretta and many other Alpha Kappa Alpha Sorority members throughout the audience. Just to be recognized by the president of the United States and singled out to stand in the presence of Oprah, Maya Angelou's family members, all other invitees, and Michelle Obama was such an honor, and I'll never forget it.

Maya Angelou is my favorite poet, so the USPS was right on point to invite me to this event. I remember so well my favorite poem by her, "Phenomenal Woman," depicting the humiliation of black people because of unfair treatment. It bolsters your confidence in being a woman and tells why you are phenomenal.

Maya Angelou won me over with her "Phenomenal Woman" poem, and I wanted to know more about her poem titled "And Still

I Rise." I read her book *I Know Why the Caged Bird Sings*, and I was so impressed with the title that once when employed at the US Department of Education, I made a card that said, "I Know Why the Caged Bird Sings," and put it outside my cubicle. As federal accountant, I had earned the opportunity to *sing* to auditors about some of the challenging accounting work I was doing. Therefore, the poem's title was significant to me.

Chapter 35

On my seventy-seventh birthday in 2018, Soror Carolyn Rowe gave me a book titled *Obama: An Intimate Portrait*, which is the definitive visual biography of Barack Obama's historic presidency captured in unprecedented detail by his White House photographer, Pete Souza. One photo shows President Obama leaning down and letting an African American boy feel his hair. The boy was in awe that his hair felt like Mr. Obama's hair. I am keeping this book of intimate photos as an heirloom to share with my family members, grandchildren, and great-grands, who will certainly read about President Obama and want to know more about him. He is history now—the first black president of America.

We must not forget that the forty-fifth president is now Donald J. Trump. Many others and I do pray that God will use him in a positive way. We know that God can use anyone to make a difference, and we pray daily that God will use him and his administration to make America continue to be great, although his campaign theme indicated he'd like to make America great again.

Chapter 36

The year 2016 brought me another treat. When I was a teacher, I had worked during one summer at the National Aeronautics and Space Administration (NASA) in Washington, DC, as a secretary in the liaison office of NASA Headquarters. This was no big-time job, but I did get to meet John Glenn, the first American to orbit the earth. My supervisor let his employees meet Mr. Glenn when he stopped by our office one afternoon.

It was a treat to see the movie *Hidden Figures* in 2016, which was the story of a team of three female African American mathematicians who served a vital role in NASA during the early years of the US space programs. The three ladies depicted were Katherine G. Johnson, Dorothy Vaughn, and Mary Jackson. All three of these ladies were members of the Alpha Kappa Alpha Sorority, Inc., although this was seldom seen in the write-ups of this film. Research, however, will bear out this fact. Of course, being an Alpha Kappa Alpha woman myself, this just inspired in me more interest in the incredible untold story of these brilliant African American women who had served as the brains behind the launch into orbit of astronaut John Glenn. In 2016, my sorority chapter had a special closed showing of this movie at a theater in Springfield, Virginia. The movie was released on December 25, 2016.

The story took place when segregation was rampant, and these African American NASA mathematicians used the segregated bathrooms instead of the "whites only" bathrooms. The African American ones were farther away from where they worked. These brilliant ladies also used separate coffeepots from those used by the whites. The story told that Katherine Johnson used the "whites only" bathrooms for years before anyone complained. When she simply ignored the complaint, the issue was dropped completely.

In 2016, Katherine Johnson was the only surviving member of the mathematical team still alive. On November 15, 2016, President Obama awarded her a Presidential Medal of Freedom for her work at NASA. Katherine Johnson, ninety-eight years old, received another honor in 2016 when a new $30 million forty-thousand-square-foot NASA building was named Katherine G. Johnson Computational Research Facility. John Glenn's launch in January 1962 specifically requested that Katherine Johnson review all the numbers for the *Friendship* 7 mission before he would agree to go through with it.

Chapter 37

I had a real problem deciding on what to do after retirement. Harmony Hall Regional Center, a community center, was close to where I lived, and I stopped by there one day to see if they had any part-time or volunteer positions. While I was talking to the gentleman at the main desk, I looked over his shoulder and saw a computer screen that displayed people exercising. I asked him, "Where is that place?"

He said, "It's the fitness center around the corner in this building." I inquired further, and he said, "It's open daily, except Sundays, from 6:30 a.m. to 9:30 p.m. If you're a Prince George's County resident and a senior citizen, you can use the fitness center for free. You can go around there and check it out if you like."

Well, there's an answer to my boredom, I thought. Now I had somewhere to go that I could enjoy each day. I'd just need to get the required ID card, and come to the fitness center. Although it wasn't the part-time job or volunteer position that had brought me to Harmony Hall Regional Center in the first place, this would work for me. After about five months, the Parks and Planning Commission employees of Harmony Hall informed us in the fitness center that a new program would begin there for seniors. It would be the Harmony Hallers' Senior Citizen Program, and Parks and

Planning was recruiting a director for this program. I became a charter member of this senior citizens' group in Fort Washington, Maryland, almost twelve years ago.

We usually have meetings on Tuesdays and Thursdays from eleven thirty in the morning to one in the afternoon. At that time, we would typically go over our activity calendar of trips, seminars, and movies for each month. We would then discuss various topics, such as scams, national and local politics, current events, voting issues, what was going on in the White House, and more.

We could join clubs such as line dancing, Zumba gold, embroidery, jewelry making, poetry club, book club, and many more, and we were able to participate in them after the regular meetings end at one o'clock. I am currently a member of the poetry and book clubs. My first day with Sylvia Dianne Beverly, also known as Lady Di, our poetry facilitator at Harmony Hall, was the first day I actually wrote a poem. I wrote this poem under the direction of Lady Di, who told us to brainstorm about faith. This was a productive activity for me, and I wrote the following on November 2, 2017:

Faith

Why do I trust God? He created heaven and earth.
My belief is anchored in the God that I trust.

He is invisible, and brings me peace and joy. If I am
patient, his strengths I, too, may implore.

All these characteristics show faith in our divine
creator. Faith the size of a mustard seed can lead to
realization of more.

I know I'm not a poet, and there is plenty of room for improvement if I continue to work with Lady Di in the poetry club. Lady Di praised our first efforts, and we gave her all the credit for our poem presentations on our first try.

The Harmony Hallers sometimes take trips to interesting places like museums, famous churches, jazz and blues concerts, and Arena Stage and other theaters, and we usually have lunch at a restaurant after each event. On Mondays, Wednesdays, and Fridays, I frequent the Fitness Center, and work out the kinks. How's that for being active all week?

Last year, in 2017, I became a charter member of the African American Museum of History and Culture in Washington, DC. Two years ago I also became a member of the Busy Bee's Bible Study Group at Grace United Methodist Church in Fort Washington, Maryland. Not only do we study the Bible, but we also unscramble word puzzles and solve other exercises to keep our brains active. Once a month we have an outing and go to various places for lunch or to the movies.

I've been a member of the Ephesian's Baptist Church in Clinton, Maryland, for eighteen years, and I currently serve as a trustee and member of the church choir. I've found that it's best for seniors to keep moving and be active on a daily basis in many facets of our lives. It's better for your physical health, and it also helps your memory functions. As a matter of fact, one of my doctors told me to get out of the house and go somewhere every day. In addition to attending meetings on Tuesdays and Thursday with the Harmony Hallers, attending Bible study classes on Wednesdays, and/or exercising at the Harmony Hall Regional Center's Fitness Center on Monday, Wednesday, and Friday, I have lunch or dinner out at various places. I also visit the library and select books to read. (Danielle Steele is my favorite author.) I make deposits at the bank for my church as a part of my trustee duties, or I sometimes go shopping at different stores. Doing activities that I like makes me happy. In other words, I try to stay busy *on purpose*. I make plans a day ahead for what I will do the next day. My life seems full of doing things that I like to do. I usually watch television in the evenings, and I use my computer several times a day to check bank balances, send emails, make bill payments, and use social media.

Chapter *38*

In July 2015, my son married a young lady named Cherelie Sarmiento Crudup from the Philippines, and they currently live with me. I told him that I had no desire to live in my five-bedroom home alone. So I have company with me at home when they are not working. On October 24, 2017, my daughter-in-law had a beautiful baby boy. They named him Daniel Sarmiento Crudup, and he is my adorable only grandchild. I just love him, and I often help babysit and teach him. Living with the three of them improves the *quality* of my life. As a seventy-seven-year-old woman, I don't have to live alone, and I have my other activities to keep me motivated, alert, and on the move.

Chapter 39

Friends and/or foes can either enhance or make your life more challenging. Since I am a very intuitive person, I know lots of people, but I pride myself on having a few solid and good friends I feel will stand by me through good times and bad. I've found that if a person is my true friend, we don't have to communicate or interact every day.

We may contact each other two, three, or maybe four times a year or whenever something especially eventful takes place and we want to talk about or do it.

My closest friend, Mrs. Alveria Grimes Griffin, lives in Portsmouth, Virginia, and we attended I. C. Norcom High School together. We took many of the same classes together. When I was twenty years old, I selected her to be my maid of honor in my church wedding. She went to Virginia State University in Petersburg, Virginia, majored in elementary education, and made a career of teaching students in their earlier years of school. I went to Norfolk State University, and made a career of teaching junior high and high school students in their secondary level of education. Although we attended different universities, we remained friends. I remember when her first son, Bernard Jr., was born. I went over to see her and Bernie Jr. and gave her a few tips on caring for him. We've never talked to each other every day, but the bond of friendship is strong. We attended our high school class reunions and made sure we saw each other. We sat together, visited the vendors, and stopped by the other events at these reunions. We were good friends through marriages, children, and reunions, but we seldom called each other—except around those times. We communicate when it's time for upcoming events. We update each other about former teachers, the success of other members of our class, or those who are sick or who have passed on. We have known how to contact each other over the years. We are staunch friends, and we have been there for each other whenever necessary, although we don't need to call each other every day or even every month. I enjoy her friendship, and I suppose we will be friends forever. At my seventy-seventh birthday party, she came up from Portsmouth to Fort Washington to be a part of it. She wrote and read to my guests many facts about my success while I was in high school and college. It's really a blessing to have such a friend who doesn't mind traveling to you to be a part of your birthday celebration.

Unfortunately, Alveria lost her husband, Bernard Sr., about five years ago, and of course, my family traveled to Portsmouth to be with her and her family. Bernard had been a student at our high school when we were there. He had served as the vice mayor of Portsmouth when he graduated. Alveria accompanied him on his many mayoral or political activities and events. She was quite a lady, and he was so proud that she was his wife. They were present at my grandmother and mother's funerals in Portsmouth and at the funerals of my in-laws when they knew my son and I would be coming to the area for family burials. Oh, what a beautiful, strong lady friend God has given me to continue blessing my life. We never need to hold back when we talk about the past, present, and the goals we have for our future. I thank God every day for giving me a true friend like her.

In the Fort Washington area, I treasure another God-given friend that I trust and can count on to help me and act in my favor. We help each other. Her family knows they are blessed to have a God-fearing woman like her as the head of their household. She, too, is a strong, intelligent young lady. Her name is Rosa Lee Cason. I met Rosa at Bolling Officer's Club in Washington, DC, at a mutual friend's retirement party. The first thing I noticed about her was that she always held her head high. We discovered that we lived about ten minutes from each other in Fort Washington. We sometimes have waited three to six months before contacting each other, but this does not lessen our friendship. When I was working, I would bring her announcements of job opportunities where I worked. She applied for one and actually got the job. Since then, she has been promoted and works at the Department of Veteran Affairs. She has proven to be a strong lady who knows what she wants and goes after it. We have been on several cruises together and with our families. She is a Christian, and she believes in treating people right. She brings alternative ideas to the table whenever we have discussions, sometimes suggesting things no one else has thought of. After twenty or more years of knowing each other, we still travel together often. She always makes sure I am well on the trips we take together. She's my favorite traveling partner and another friend who will do anything she can for me. She knows that I look out for her as well. *Thank you, God, for blessing me with another friend who is as close as family.*

Another friend who is a Christian and does all she can for friends and family is Janice Boss. I met Janice when I worked at the US Department of Education. We became work friends at the department, and we shared many common interests.

We became friends since we were both new to the office. We started talking about our families, and then we started having lunch together. We shared handyman contacts and information that was good to know.

Janice definitely has an entrepreneurial spirit and likes to try to sell different products. She was very helpful to me when I was a Shaklee health product salesperson. With her help, I had enough sales to increase my clientele and income, and I became a Shaklee director in less than a year in this program. We had fun setting up interest meetings at various places and introducing many to the advantages of using our Shaklee products. She soon became a Shaklee distributor. She moved on to working with many makeup products, and she is now marketing another new and different product. She believes in her product, and she has been very successful in increasing her income in this area. She is a hard worker.

Janice and I have taken trips together with a social club in Maryland, and we have also been on cruises together. She is an avid church member, and like me, she sings in the choir. She is author of a book as well. Janice is active in other organizations. She has also held the highest position in Blacks in Government (BIG). One common factor among my close friends is that they are Christian women who stay on the move. When we do get together, we always have a lot of information to share.

I do have two special family friends I would put in the close friends category because they have shown concern for me, my health, and my interests. They are my sisters-in-law. We are in contact with one another often. I know I can call on them whenever necessary, and I can count on their help in any situation.

As for foes, I would say that you should expect to have a few, whether or not you have done anything to deserve them. You can usually tell if someone doesn't want you as a friend. In this case, I just try to surround myself with positive and successful people, enjoy and learn from them, and keep on moving and enjoying life.

Chapter *40*

I set goals for my life. Setting goals helps us to stay focused and maintain a purpose for activities in which we direct our attention. One of my goals for the future is to keep my strong faith in God and come to a realization of why God has kept me here all these years. Yes, I need to realize my purposes for living. All of us are put here for a reason, and when God feels we have accomplished this, he will call us home. Teaching is a gift from God. I know I was meant to teach, whether in a classroom or not. I've served this purpose in a classroom for twenty years. But there are other ways to teach, either by example or purposefully tutoring adults or children who need extra help to be successful in their endeavors.

As a student, I actually took a class in charm. This was so helpful to me in improving my social skills and demeanor. I plan to offer a similar class in charm for students I think would benefit from it—say in early grade levels. This is one of my goals for helping and giving back to young children. Of course, I will work with preschoolers too.

I plan to elevate my writing skills to the point that I can successfully use my imagination to write any type of novel. I want to use my skills to maintain alertness as I continue to mature.

I plan to help children by tutoring community youth in mathematics and English and by also helping them improve their reading skills. I am a very quiet person, but I'm also very observant. I plan to be more vocal and active in the organizations in which I have membership.

These are just a few goals I've set for my future to remain active … *on purpose.*

Chapter *41*

If asked to describe my life's journey thus far, I would say it's been an amazing uphill/downhill journey influenced positively by God, who's definitely taken over my heart and soul. I've been handicapped many times by the devil trying to gain control of me and keep me moving downhill. I am grateful to God for His guidance and blessings in helping me overcome the setbacks and for the miracles He's worked in my life. I ask for His continued grace and favor in the years to come. On New Year's Day 2018, I asked God to continue to bless me so that I can be a blessing to others. I believe God will save you if you believe and confess to Him your sins, ask for His forgiveness, and then repent. I need to take a look at my enjoyment of casinos, especially the slot machines, as this is one area that has no religious purpose. I ask my friends to pray for me in this regard. I do want to be ready when God calls me to leave this earth and come on up to heaven to be with Him and to see my loved ones again. I can't imagine anything more inviting and glorious. I believe God has been keeping me alive and is saving me to help and teach many generations—the ones I've taught in the past, present, and those to come. This will include my grandchildren and great-grandchildren and maybe even some of yours. I've journalized my accomplishments to give hope to the hopeless and to encourage all to let God use them to spread His goodness and His Word. I know there is a God because He has revealed his powers and miracles to me. Sometimes this revelation may come through His acts and blessings in the lives of others. Now I just want to tell of His goodness to me and encourage others to accept Him as their Savior and thus defeat the devil in their lives. Only God can and will do this. He's also promised never to leave us. This is my greatest testimony! He can open doors that have been shut and shut doors that have been open.

Chapter *42*

M editation is important to energize our spirit and bring peace to our minds. I meditate at night before retiring to reflect on all the blessings I received that day. I do this as soon as I wake up in the morning to prepare and ready myself for what I may face during the new day. Thoughts that work for inspiring me and energizing my spirit are mainly scriptural, although there are other sources for inspiration. Some I get from listening to inspirational speakers and reading other books, and sometimes the outcomes of movies may stir me. We can reflect and meditate on numerous Bible verses as sources of comfort. So too, inspirational writings, motivational speakers, sermons, and hymns can serve to encourage and strengthen my faith in God. It is my hope that they will nourish and speak to your heart and spirit and bring you a sense of purpose, peace, and comfort in your life as well. Just try them instead of feeling depressed or hopeless in life. Make a real effort to help yourself in life.

There are many hymns for inspiration and meditation. Some that I enjoy—and I hope that you will enjoy them as well—are as follows: "My God Is Real," "Total Praise," "How Great Thou Art," "My God Is an Awesome God," "God Will Take Care of You," "My Father Watches Over Me," "My God Is Awesome," and "Precious Lord, Take My Hand." But we know there are many more. If we believe in God, just looking at the title of the hymn sometimes can give us renewed inspiration.

Some inspirational poems on which I reflect include "Still I Rise" and "Phenomenal Woman" by Maya Angelou and "Footprints in the Sand" by Mary Fishback Powers. These poems have inspired me when I've gone through my toughest times, and they have inspired millions.

I truly thank God for carrying me through poetic inspiration so many times in my life!

Inspirational Messages of Pastor

Photo by Deacon Bobby Jones

The following is a message for meditation, unpublished and penned just for Christian reflection and other purposes as a favor to me. I feel it's awesome, and therefore, I want to share it with you. Enjoy!

A Meditation on Evil in God's Good Creation
Rev. Anton T. Wesley, M.Div.
Pastor, Ephesians Baptist Church
Clinton, Maryland

Adam and Eve, although created holy and sinless from the hand of God (created in His image and after His likeness), fell from grace because of Adam intentionally transgressing the one law that he was told to observe. Evil personified by the serpent tempted Adam with a quick and easy path to what he thought was a truer and fuller equality with God. Adam's transgression was not a rebellion against God, whom he loved, but rather an attempt to become even more godlike than he already was. His sin lay in his unwillingness to trust God's judgment rather than his own about what he was spiritually mature enough to handle. We know that he was wrong to think this way, yet we continue to this very day to make similar errors.

Why did not God simply wipe evil from the world? If the angels with flaming swords were able to keep Adam and Eve from going back into the garden, then it stands to reason that angels could have prevented the serpent from entering the garden in the first place. Why does God permit evil to flourish? I believe the answer lies in the power of the human mind to choose. For reasons fully known only to God, humanity must be permitted the right of choice. God wants our love, loyalty, devotion, and so forth, but He also wants us to freely choose, to want to give Him those things. However, we cannot truly and fully choose to want to do them unless we have a real option not to do them. We cannot truly choose to love and honor God and what is good unless we are intimately aware of evil and have the option to embrace evil rather than God. We must choose to hate evil. We must learn from this bitter and painful experience.

If we are to be truly godlike, then we must mimic Him in every way that we can, and that includes mimicking the way that God eternally chooses to be good. We have the power of choice precisely because God does. God chooses to be good, and He always has done so. God is pure, infinite intellect. The devil is not infinite. So God could easily outdevil the devil if He chose to. Thank God that He does not choose this. His divine nature is so infinitely good as to render an evil choice never possible. We are praiseworthy and deserving of reward when we exercise our God-given right to choose by choosing to really choose as God Himself chooses. We Christians know that evil exists in the presence of a perfect and holy God. Choosing to be godlike by choosing to be good and godly in this wicked world gives glory to God. May God evermore be glorified.

Chapter 43

I have been through so much. I've dusted myself off many times and continued on my journey only by the grace of the Lord. The devil has followed me around and tried to keep me too sick to function. From my prayers and those of my family members (especially Mama Minnie), God has blessed me with success in many ways. I've set goals, and through meditation and reflection, I've been inspired in my journey. I asked some people in my life how they see me now. Is there something they especially remember about me? Some of their responses follow, and these let me know that I am on the right path for God's purpose. I know I can fight any kind of depression. Through his grace, he keeps me stable. I'm so grateful!

Clarice Burthey Crudup is a lovely Christian lady on the outside, but more importantly, she has a beautiful spirit on the inside. Her smile is contagious, and she carries herself like an elegant and well-dressed refined lady. I met Clarice a few years ago at the Harmony Hall Senior Center in Fort Washington, Maryland, where she is a charter member. We became very good friends. Also, Clarice has so graciously supported my first book, and I really appreciated her support. After a few conversations, I shared with her that "she should write a book about her life, her sicknesses, her family, her walk with the Lord, and the many miracles she experienced in her life."

Her personal story will inspire you to want to and do your very best each day. I am very honored to know Clarice and happy to call her my dear friend.

—Joyce Williams-Graves, author and poet

Clarice and I met in the eighth grade in the fifties when she relocated to my hometown, Portsmouth, Virginia. We clicked immediately and became fast friends. Her demeanor has always been calm, ladylike, easygoing, in control, and quite congenial.

My dear friend and I have been close for more than sixty years. As her friend, I am so very delighted and grateful that she is enjoying the state of mind that she is experiencing at this time in her life. I encourage her to persevere. May the Almighty bless you abundantly, Clarice, and keep you in His care.

—Alveria Griffin, friend

I recently met Clarice around January 2017 when I retired from the federal government and joined the Harmony Haller Senior Program. Ms. Clarice was very nice to me, and we hit it off very quickly. Ms. Clarice is a very fashionable and warm person. Clarice loves her family and her new grandson. May God bless her.

—Mrs. Margaret Vanzego, Harmony Haller

I met Clarice in 1994 at a mutual friend's retirement luncheon. We sat next to each other and opened up a dialogue. It was an instant friendship to this day. I remember I was in search of a job at the time. I asked her if they were hiring at ED. She said yes. The very next day she faxed me a job announcement within ED. I did get the job, by the way.

Clarice introduced me to travel, more than I had been, although I had just retired from the navy. For more than twenty years, I attended her AKA luncheons. I could not have chosen a better friend.

—Ms. Rosa Lee Cason, friend

Photo by Deacon Bobby Jones

I have been the pastor of Sister Crudup for at least eighteen years. She is one of the founding members of Ephesians Baptist Church of Clinton, Maryland, of which it is my privilege to be the founding pastor. Her love for her church family is expressed often as she distributes hugs and thoughtful comments to each of us. She is a dignified woman who carries herself with elegance and class. She serves her church as a member of the board of trustees and she also sings in the choir. She supports her church financially as well. Her warmth, cordiality, and Christian deportment are an inspiration to all who know her. God bless you to climb higher, Sister Crudup!

—Rev. Anton T. Wesley

One of my favorite customers is Mrs. Clarice. She is a classy lady. She seems to enjoy life. She's always on time for her appointments. You see—I'm her hairstylist. I find her really easy to talk to. She's intelligent and well spoken. She's confident with an enthusiastic outlook on life.

—Mrs. Sadie Risby, hairstylist

She has two names—Mrs. Crudup and Sister Crudup. Read the following to understand the reason for this distinction.

Mrs. Crudup: I was sixteen years old at the time and sitting in her classroom for the first time in my high school in Arlington, Virginia. She wrote her name on the board and said, "I'm Mrs. Crudup, and I will be teaching you business/vocational training." Her voice was soft but stern. She was very classy, demanding respect and giving respect to those who approached her. She dressed very elegantly as a schoolteacher. I was proud to see her each day, knowing that I too one day would have a job where people would respect me and knowing that dressing for the occasion is also important. Clothes do make the woman. She taught me what I needed to know to get a good job in a business environment. She helped to make me what I am to this day.

As time went on, I became an executive assistant for one of the top firms in the nation. I owe all of that to teachers like Mrs. Crudup.

Sister Crudup: One day at church, I looked around the congregation and saw this woman sitting a few pews in front of me with a wide-brim hat on and everything matching from head to toe. It was Mrs. Crudup. As time went on, we became trustees in our church, working side by side for our Lord. We also had to collect the offerings. I remember having to pray over the offerings, and Sister Crudup could tell I was nervous. She pulled me aside and told me, "Just start by giving thanks to God first. Then let God do the rest." And it worked! She was my angel that day. Thank you, Sister Crudup, for being there for me all these years. I will always cherish our friendship.

—Sister Alease Turner, church trustee

Soror Clarice is my Alpha Kappa Alpha Sorority sister, and I have known her for several years. I was her buddy, and we rode to meetings and other chapter activities together. During this time, she provided me with motherly words of advice. I also discovered that she is a God-fearing sister in Christ. The fact that her son is so committed to her and the church as a deacon speaks volumes about her as a mother!

Soror Clarice is also a doting grandmother. Not only is she a wonderful grandmother; she is a glamorous grandmother. My life has been enriched by knowing this woman of God.

—Martha Coleman, sorority sister

I first met Clarice when we were freshmen at Norfolk State University. Throughout our college years, we were close friends. I was a bridesmaid in her wedding.

After graduation Clarice and Cleveland moved to Northern Virginia, where she had gotten a teaching job, and Jim and I joined the Peace Corps. Clarice and I stayed in touch, and after serving in the Peace Corps, we moved to Northern Virginia too. Clarice had joined Alpha Kappa Alpha Sorority Inc. and she later sponsored me, which drew us even closer to each other.

Clarice has had her share of trials and tribulations. Today I see Clarice as an overcomer. She is a strong Christian woman with great faith in God. She is a dear, sweet friend of fifty-nine years.

—Regina Crawley, sorority sister

I met my now soror, friend, and mentor as a customer many years ago. Over time, we became great friends. Every time she came in, she entered with confidence, and she had a light about her. We spoke at length about the sorority and my interest. She invited me to various events, and I was eventually initiated into the very same chapter. Almost ten years later, she is still one of my favorite people. I hope she knows how much of an impact she's made in the lives of me and others around her.

—Delvina Offer, sorority sister

Beliefs That Keep Me at Peace

Some of the personal beliefs I cling to for hope and guidance since I've been traveling with God in spite of the devil being around and trying to make me unsuccessful and unbelieving include the following:

1. Here's a *key* belief: God so loved the world that He sent His only begotten Son so that whosoever believes in Him shall not perish but shall have everlasting life.
2. Jesus died on the cross for our sins. This is a compassionate and unselfish thing.
3. God has shown me favor in handling problems in my life. He has given me many opportunities and positive outcomes.
4. I should respect that favor and adhere to His holy words and deeds. I strive to do this most of the time.
5. God will never leave me alone. My Savior is always there for me.
6. I should pray to Him, always believing that He can and will grant what I'm praying to Him for. My pastor stresses this very often in his sermons.
7. I will be destined for hell if I do not follow the Ten Commandments—unless I ask forgiveness, believing that He will forgive me, and then repent for any sins I commit. This was ingrained in me by my father at an early age.
8. You should love your neighbor just as you love yourself. I strive to do something nice for at least one person every single day.
9. I believe that God's almighty mercy and power is available to all who follow Him. Since they're available to me, I believe these are available to all.
10. I can do all things through Christ because He strengthens me. This belief has been proven to me time and time again as I go through life.

What's next in my journey with Christ Jesus? Only God knows His future plans for me; however, I plan to continue to keep God first in my life by praying, meditating, being guided by the Holy Spirit and inspirational messages, associating with positive people, and trying to be a blessing to others. We're all imperfect creatures. If I should sin through weakness, I will pray to God for forgiveness and repent for my sins. God has healed me from depression in my life. I remain well because Jesus is with me on my journey. With His continued blessings and His grace and mercy, I believe the *best* is yet to come. Amen!

About the Author

C larice Burthey Crudup was born in Durham, North Carolina. She graduated with honors from I. C. Norcom High School in Portsmouth, Virginia, in 1958. She graduated from Norfolk State University and received a bachelor's degree in business education in 1962. She was the salutatorian of the university's graduating class in 1962. She also took classes in economics at George Washington University in Washington, DC.

Clarice retired from two careers—teaching after twenty years and working for the federal government after another twenty years. She is a Golden soror with more than fifty years of membership in Northern Virginia's Zeta Chi Omega chapter of Alpha Kappa Alpha Sorority, Inc. This is the first book she has written. She has one son, a daughter-in-law, and a grandson.

Clarice currently lives with her family in Fort Washington, Maryland.

Printed in the United States
By Bookmasters